A MYSTERY

TAMPERING WITH EVIDENCE

FRANCES APPLEQUIST

World Castle Publishing, LLC
Pensacola, Florida
Copyright © Frances Applequist 2022
Paperback ISBN: 9781956788709
eBook ISBN: 9781956788716
First Edition World Castle Publishing, LLC, March 29, 2022
http://www.worldcastlepublishing.com

Cover: Karen Fuller
Editor: Maxine Bringenberg

PROLOGUE
THE DISCOVERY

A skeletal hand and wrist appeared above the wet embankment, poking out of emerging green and what was left of the brown leaves. Its fingers reached toward her. Threatening? Pleading? Warning?

Jenna Rossi gasped and fell backward against a tall oak tree. On trembling legs, she slid to its base and landed hard among roots and leaves. Unaware of the damp earth soaking her jeans and unable to think, she stared wide-eyed and perspiring in the cool spring morning.

Unmarked, time passed. Only two questions formed: *Who are you,* and *who put you here*? Since eight generations of the MacKenna family had owned this estate, Jenna glanced heavenward and asked, "Kathleen! Did you know about this?"

Jenna's memory of her friend screamed back at her, *NO!*

Jenna stared toward the Victorian house hidden by the forest. Then she studied the woods around her and wondered, *With over nine hundred acres to choose from, why bury you this close to the stream bank?* She stared at the ragged rim of earth that slid down to the wide, fast stream. Her organized mind snapped back to clarity, and she understood. "You," she said aloud, "were not buried this close to the stream back then."

She stood and stared toward the estate road, hidden by distance and trees. "Maybe your grave digger couldn't carry you farther." *Yes, she thought, the only roads deeper into the estate go past the house, and they're little more than dirt trails.* "Almost impossible at night," she said aloud, and repeated, "At night."

The police. I need to call the police. Sergeant Harley's a good guy. Her inner voice cried, *No. I might be calling the police on Kathleen, or Ronan, or Liam, or Finn.* The fact that they were all dead made it worse. They were not there to defend themselves. *No police,* she thought, *not yet.*

CHAPTER 1
OPENED ENDINGS

Kathleen, the last of the MacKenna clan, had died three weeks earlier, and Jenna always remembered that day as though she were reliving it.

Kathleen's twenty-year-old maid, Aida, had called Jenna, crying. "Please come, Miss Jenna. Miss Kathleen's fightin' with the doctor, again, and I'm scared for her!"

Jenna had thrown a light wrap over her nightgown and sped to the old Victorian house. She used her key and ran up the familiar steps to the second floor.

Aida sat in the back corner of the shadowy room. Her black uniform made her all but invisible. Only the fireplace glow reflected in the girl's golden eyes gave her position away.

A fire, seventy-eight degrees on the thermostat, and heavy drapes stifled the room. The young doctor perspired while Kathleen lay shrouded in blankets and shivering.

In a soft voice, Jenna said, "Excuse me."

The doctor flinched.

"I'm Jenna Rossi, a friend of Miss Kathleen's."

The doctor assessed her small frame and pixie haircut and said, "Good. Then you can convince Mrs. MacKenna that the best place for her is in hospice."

Jenna frowned and asked, "And what will they do for her there?"

The doctor assured the two women, "They'll help her."

Eyes narrowed, tone sharp, Jenna asked, "And they'll restore her health?"

The young doctor's face flushed. In a tight voice, he said, "Mrs. MacKenna is seventy-nine years old and ill. Restoring her health is impossible, but they can manage her pain."

Jenna softened her voice and asked her

friend, "Are you in a lot of pain, Kathleen? Do you want the hospital?"

The old woman wrinkled her nose and gasped the phrases, "Strange bed. Cold room. Nurses waking me every time I fall asleep. A damned monitor ticking off my last minutes. By the saints, no!"

"Ms. Rossi," the doctor snapped, "my patient does not have time for this."

Jenna moved past the doctor to Kathleen's side. She stroked the white hair that was once thick and fiery red. She stared into the watery eyes that were once emerald green. Swallowing hard, she asked, "Kathleen? Do you want to risk dying sooner if you stay here?"

From the corner, Aida gasped.

The doctor interrupted, but Jenna cut him off with, "Kathleen. It's your life: your choice."

Through cracked lips, the old woman sputtered, "He's not my doctor, Jenna. I don't know him, and I'll only be leavin' my home for my grave."

Jenna faced the doctor. "Aida and I are witnesses to Miss Kathleen's intention to stay," she said. "If you've called an ambulance, cancel it."

The doctor opened his mouth but closed it fast.

Before he recovered, Jenna asked, "You're the son of her regular physician, aren't you?" Not waiting for an answer, she added, "So, I suggest you call your father for his opinion. I'm sure Miss Kathleen won't mind if you used the phone on the landing."

The doctor left, and Jenna went back to Kathleen. She touched her cheek and assured her, "I'm doing what I can to help you end this where you want." She saw relief in her old friend's eyes.

The doctor returned and handed a bottle of pills to Jenna. "For pain," he said, and left. This time they heard his footfalls on the stairs and the heavy front door open and close.

Jenna turned to Kathleen and asked, "Do you want anything for pain?"

"No! It'll only fluther away the last of me."

Laughing, Jenna asked, "Okay. You want company or rest?"

With effort, Kathleen breathed out, "Ah,

visitin' would be grand, don't-cha know?"

Jenna turned to Aida and asked. " Do you mind bringing sweet tea — and one for yourself if you'd like to stay with us."

"Yes, ma'am," the young woman answered, leaving for the kitchen.

Jenna hoped the shy young woman would join them.

Faster than expected, Aida returned with a tray. On it was a pitcher of water they had not requested and three chilled glasses of sweet tea. The girl settled into the chair farthest from the fire.

The late hour and the shadowy room kindled Jenna's memories. She began telling Kathleen just what their friendship meant to her.

Jenna's voice sent them all back in time to the years when Kathleen's sons — Jenna's friends — were still alive, and the old house vibrated with the laughter of teenagers. In the glow of the bedside lamp, Jenna drew vibrant word pictures of Christmas parties, fireside chats, late-night snacks in Kathleen's kitchen, and formal meals in her dining room. In specific places in each story, she tried to imitate the heavy brogue of a younger, more vital Kathleen. She was terrible at it, but her efforts made Kathleen laugh: short and wheezy, and wonderful to hear.

Kathleen's cloudy eyes cleared, and her ragged breathing evened out. She smiled and said, "I better not linger too long, darlings. I need to be at heaven's gate an hour before the devil knows I'm dead!"

Laughing, Jenna shared memories for another half-hour. After the last sip of her sweet tea, she said, "Rest now, Kathleen. I'll visit again in the morning." Jenna leaned over to kiss her friend and saw that Kathleen's eyes had closed. Her old friend had stopped breathing.

Aida came out of her chair with her hand in front of her mouth. She stared at Kathleen with large eyes. Trembling, she asked, "Is she gone?"

Police and people from the coroner's office controlled the rest of the night. Jenna and Aida did their best to answer an exhausting string of questions.

The next thing Jenna did was go with Aida to the young woman's bedroom and tuck her in as though she were a child. Then she pulled the heavy draperies against the morning sun. The last thing she did was curl up on the loveseat near the bed, not wanting to leave Aida alone. Everything that came after that night happened fast.

On the day of the funeral, few people came. Kathleen's dignified and sad lawyer stood with her teary-eyed doctor and his distracted son. Several black-veiled locals came to celebrate the passing of someone they openly envied.

I wish they didn't have the satisfaction, Jenna thought, *of another MacKenna tragedy to gossip about.* She closed her eyes, chastising herself for her judgements.

Later that day, Kathleen's lawyer read the will to only Jenna and Aida. He also gave Jenna a letter. Because it was in Kathleen's shaky hand, it must have been written at least five years before, when Kathleen could still write. It said:

My Dearest Jenna,

I have only three requests.

First, find a way to keep the house in your family. Leave it to the son who loves it most. Second, please breathe your life into the old place. My sweet husband, my boys, me — none of us ever resisted an estate sale. They were our sport and our obsessions. But you, my dear, have that demon need to be neat. Sell whatever you want to pay for the preservation of the rest. Third, and most important to me, if you or your boys must sell land, please keep a one-hundred-acre square of woods around the house. I can't bear the thought of the world crowding it in.

Love, Kathleen

P.S.: When you are ready, call the auctioneer, Sam Lester. I've bought enough from him to trust him.

The lawyer went on to explain that Kathleen had established a trust to pay taxes on the estate. She also left a few thousand dollars to Aida, along with the 1958 Cadillac the young woman had used to chauffer Kathleen around town.

Alarmed, Jenna realized that Kathleen did not have the assets to give Aida enough. The young, uneducated, out of work, now homeless woman needed more than a few thousand dollars to restart her life.

When Jenna had a moment alone with her, she asked, "When I move into the Victorian, do you want to take over the lease on my apartment? You can have most of the furniture, and I'll keep paying the rent for two months to give you time to find work."

Aida had stared at Jenna and asked, "Really?"

"Yes. I'll try to work it out with the landlord."

Speechless, the young woman nodded her assent.

After the funeral, Jenna had spent the next week swapping homes with Aida. The single mother of three teenagers paid the next two months' rent on Aida's apartment and helped her young friend search want ads for jobs that only needed a high school education.

A week later, Aida and Jenna sat at the

round table in the younger woman's small kitchen. Aida folded her newspaper, and Jenna closed her laptop. Undaunted, Aida ignored their failed search and said, "Wow. This is the first place I've ever had that's mine, ever! How can I thank you?"

"It's not a fair trade."

"Miss Kathleen gave me a safe place to live and helped me with my elementary and high school homework, but that didn't make the Victorian mine or make her my mother. You're as much one of her children as her own sons—God rest their souls—so the will's better than fair; it's right."

Jenna squinted at the younger woman and asked, "Had you two talked about it?"

Aida smiled and cooed, "Now, Miss Jenna, you aren't really asking me to break a confidence, are you?"

"No. I guess I'm not."

The young woman, who made a T-shirt and jeans look like a fashion statement, said, "I really have a place that's mine!"

"Yours and the landlord's. I've talked to my sons, and they agree. Sell things, move things, change stuff, paint…do whatever you want within the rules of the lease."

"Thank your boys for me."

Mention of her boys reminded Jenna of Kathleen's Liam and Finn. Jenna had been only a little younger than them when they died. She and Kathleen had held each other when they cried and shared a long and agonizing period of grief. Yet Jenna never understood the depth of Kathleen's grief until she had sons of her own to lose.

***

Having caught up to the present, Jenna glared at the skeletal hand in front of her. "What are you reaching for?" she asked. Then she leaned back against a tree, shuddered, and groaned. "Well, Kathleen, the Victorian and almost a thousand acres of forest are a breathtaking gift, but the skeleton? Not so much." A sharp jab of guilt dove deep into her chest as she thought, *Ungrateful. Sorry, my friend.* "Still," she said aloud, *the house has its challenges.*

Although the inheritance was mortgage free with a trust to pay the taxes, the Victorian needed major repairs. It was also crammed from basement to rafters with STUFF that made it hard for Jenna to breathe. Claustrophobia: Kathleen had always called it Jenna's "demon."

Jenna glared at the boney hand. It was within the requested one-hundred-acre perimeter. "Oh, Kathleen," she sighed. Jenna moved away from the skeleton but did not leave. The thing to do was to find out how old it was. As a counselor at University High School, she had access to the science lab, but was clueless about the equipment.

Intending to use her pocketknife — a gift from her son, Michael — to snip a piece of fabric, she inched closer. That's when she noticed the cufflink hanging by a few threads and mused, *Nylon or a polymer blend. Cotton would have disintegrated — and I'll assume it's a man.* Gently and carefully, Jenna clipped the threads and plucked the cufflink. Then she snipped a piece of the heavy jacket and the shirt. Staring at the objects in her hand, she wondered, *Just how many laws can I break in a day? This must be several of them.* Jenna had been stupid often enough in the past to recognize the current stomach crunch as an indication.

I should call the police, she thought. Then she yelled skyward, "Kathleen! Whether you put this here or not, you will hate what comes next!" *Investigators*, Jenna thought, *trampling over the grounds and tearing through the house — and Kathleen's life.*

Jenna imagined the shell-shocked faces of the first investigators who stepped through the front door of the Victorian, and she smiled. Then she imagined them upending everything, and she frowned.

Thinking about the end of her sons' college semesters, Jenna frowned again. The oldest, Marcus, and the twins, Michael and Anthony, were coming home for the summer, and she did not want them stumbling onto their boney inheritance. She arranged branches and leaves to hide the hand and forearm, checking and double-checking to make sure the foliage looked natural.

She had just returned to the house when the phone rang. With stomach-pinching cheerfulness, the woman on the other end said, "Jenna! Remember me? It's Carol Ann Abbott."

Cautiously, Jenna said, "Good morning, Carol Ann, how are you?" She settled into a club chair to half listen to the light-hearted ramblings of her former friend.

A voice change told her that Carol Ann had reached her point. "We're calling about Kathleen," the woman said, "and I just can't tell you how sad Billy and I are. That woman made some warm memories for us in that sweet little house of hers."

The disingenuous labeling of the large Victorian as a "sweet little house" alerted Jenna.

"Well, we were delighted that she left the place to y'all; she always did row with both oars. After all, you stuck by her when that horrid accident destroyed…her family."

Carol Ann's referring to Ronan and his sons, in a ploy to get the house, gave Jenna an instant headache, but she remained silent.

Carol Ann's voice softened. With a slight tremor, she added, "I hope she understood that I didn't know how to deal with losing them. I wanted to go to the funeral alone to stand by her, but I just couldn't get myself there without my

Billy. He's always been my rock. Afterwards, I fell apart. You're different, Jenna. Ma always said I was 'icing with no cake,' while you were 'cake with no icing.'

"Anyway, Billy and I know that, despite y'all trying to help Kathleen keep up to small repairs, the house needs major work, doesn't it? Pardon me for my bluntness, but — bless your heart — your little inheritance is both a gift and a burden, isn't it?"

Jenna did not answer and waited for the snap.

"Well, Billy and I have a successful real estate business, and we can help you sell off land, and even the house — anything to give you and your sons an easy life. Why don't Billy and I just come talk to you about it?"

Jenna came back with, "I'm still sorting through Kathleen's affairs, but if we decide to sell, I'll call you. Right now, I'm needed in the kitchen. I'm sure we'll see each other soon. Bye, Carol Ann." Jenna hung up. She closed her eyes and breathed deep for a minute. Her rudeness had been a necessary defense against the assault on her nerves.

Shrugging off her former friend's greed, Jenna carried the cufflink and small swatches of fabric into Kathleen's kitchen. She held them under a light spray of warm water, watching the dirt flow away from them. One swatch turned out to be faded brown leather. The other was a light green nylon. She laid the swatches between paper towels and pressed out excess water. Next, she cleaned the cufflink, dried it, and laid it by the fabrics. It was made from a silver coin on which a large man stood between two women. Jenna read the words, Liberte, Egalite, and the last word, Fraternite. She guessed it meant liberty, equality, and fraternity. On the back, the words Republique Francaise arched around a wreath with Fifty Francs printed in the center. "Were you French?" she asked the skeleton. *No,* she told herself, *the coin could have been bought by anyone in any novelty or coin shop, anywhere in the world, and any time after it was minted.* Jenna sighed and turned away from the artifacts.

Needing to focus on a more solvable problem, she thought about the house. All the tiles, fixtures, and appliances in the house were white. All the fireplaces were white marble. All the floors, except the tiled bathrooms, had dark, oak planking. She wanted to keep all that. Her major problem was that Kathleen and at least four generations of her family had been packrats.

CHAPTER 2
TRANSITIONS

The next several evenings, while Aida rearranged her apartment cabinets and scanned want ads, Jenna sat with the estate lawyer and interviewed antique dealers. Waves of nausea hit her in unexpected moments, but she kept telling herself, "I can do anything I have to do."

Kathleen had recommended the auctioneer, Sam Lester. Jenna would wait to call him until she knew what she wanted to keep, gift, and sell. Her claustrophobia and obsession with cleanliness made owning Kathleen's clutter nerve rattling. Owning a dead body made it worse. She thought about the police again but said, *No. It will be too easy for them to blame Kathleen or her family.*

Jenna made time to study the fabric she had taken from the skeleton and realized that a leather jacket might have had wool or fleece inside that would have been eaten away long ago. *I need to go back out there and search for more clues.* A chill ran from her toes up through her spine. She shook her head and called out to the skeleton, "No. You have to wait." Then she raised her eyes toward the sky beyond the ceilings and groaned, "Kathleen, you knew how claustrophobic I am. You knew I'd have to clean this out to live here. Why didn't you talk to me about all this?"

She imagined her friend saying, "Ah, Lass, do what you need to be doin' to the parts to love the whole. Get 'fluthered' if you need to — and you know that means drunk, don't-cha, darlin'?"

Jenna went into the kitchen, where she poured Emmet's Irish Crème into a cocktail glass instead of a cordial glass. On such an overwhelming project, what mattered most was getting started. Finding a pen without finding a pad, she used a paper towel to make a quick list of the keepers: crystal, silver, bone china, Wedgewood, ivory, and jade.

The following weekend, she tackled the dining room. She decided to keep the pearl-gray wall color, long black walnut table, and twelve high-backed chairs. She remembered Kathleen saying, "Ah, darlin'. A well-padded chair's like a well-padded man, easy on old bones."

Jenna emptied the contents of the walnut breakfront and three mismatched curio cabinets onto the dining room table. Using her napkin list of keepers, she cleaned, sorted, and organized the pieces. Crystal bowls went in one curio cabinet, Wedgewood and Chinese tea sets in the second, and the silver coffee set with other silver items in the third. Bone china dishes and crystal glassware went in the breakfront with the largest matching set of silverware. The dining room table still sagged under the weight of what she did not want.

Exhausted, Jenna collapsed on a chair and telephoned Aida. After a deep breath, she said, "Hi, honey. It's Jenna. I've finished the dining room. Do you want to see what I set aside to gift or sell?"

"Yes, thank you."

Jenna asked, "When can you come?" then remembered to add, "Oh, and the things we left in the apartment, you can make a little money by selling what you don't want."

After they set a time to meet, Jenna showered and got ready for bed. Unwilling to use Kathleen's bedroom, she went into a guest room she had cleaned for herself. She crawled under the covers. A heartbeat later, she slipped into a black void where she reached out but touched nothing.

Suddenly, a white skeletal hand darted from the pitch, grabbing for her throat. She jerked backward, propelling herself through the blackness. The hand darted forward and grabbed hold of her. It was bone but implausibly slimy and cold. Wrenching loose, Jenna recoiled into an uncontrolled spin. She screamed and struggled to awaken, but the dream held her. The hand attacked again. Shivering and perspiring, she crashed through a ceiling of ice into daylight.

Awake and upright, the overcrowded

room closed in on her. She gasped for air. Her mind raced, repeating the thought, *I can't breathe in this house!* Jenna rolled her shoulders to unknot them. *I need to focus on things I can do. I need control.* She stared through the bedroom window toward the skeleton. "You have to wait," she snapped, "because I don't know what to do about you!" Jenna pulled the covers tighter around herself. "But I can fix this house," she said aloud. *That's something I know how to do.* She repeated the mantra, "I can do this. I can do this," until she slipped into darkness and found herself buried inside a curio cabinet. As she flailed at the glass, it cracked, letting gritty dirt seep through onto her face and into her nose and mouth. She jumped out of the dream, shoving away her covers and choking. Soaked in perspiration, she did not want to sleep again. She gave up and left her bed to take a shower.

Afterward, she made herself a strong cup of coffee and settled down to search the Internet for a cufflink or a coin that matched the one from the skeleton. She had not realized how long she worked until the clanking doorknocker startled her. She wrapped the cufflink and hid it in her pocket before running to open the door for her visitor.

"Hi, Aida! Next time, come in and call out, 'I'm here!' That's what I've been doing for thirty years."

"Miss Jenna, I don't think I can do that."

"We've known each other for eight years. Can we drop the Miss Jenna and Miss Aida when we're together? I honestly don't have enough energy for extra syllables."

Aida laughed and said, "It'll take some getting used to."

"We'll work on it. Come on into the dining room. It's the only room I've done so far."

Jenna had an empty box waiting by the dining room table. Making fast choices, Aida selected a few dishes, glasses, and bric-a-brac. The different prints were all florals.

Jenna loved having sons, but working with Aida gave her an idea of what it might have been like to have a daughter. When they were finished, Jenna said, "I'll call you when I've found more that I can share."

"Yes, thank you. But Miss Kathleen

wanted you and your sons to have it all."

Jenna laughed, saying, "She left me more than I can live with." A vision of the skeleton flashed in front of her, and she thought, *Aida lived here for eight years and could have found it!* A wave of nausea passed through the older woman.

"You okay, Miss Jenna?"

"Just tired, so I'll rest when we're done."

The two women packed Aida's box into the old Cadillac, and the younger woman left.

Back in the kitchen, Jenna refreshed her coffee and returned to her online search for a match to the cufflink. Five minutes later, the phone rang. The lawyer had something else for her to sign, so she drove into town.

For the next four nights, Jenna told herself she needed to breathe more than she needed to help a long-dead stranger. After work, she dedicated herself to cleaning out the kitchen.

That Saturday, Aida came again. Surveying the restocked dining room table, the young woman mused, "I never understood why Miss Kathleen needed nine potato peelers and ten cutting boards. Did her parents or grandparents, or great-grandparents, have that many servants making supper?"

Jenna shook her head and answered, "Garage sales, flea markets, estate sales — collecting was a MacKenna family hobby. I have no idea what was really left by Kathleen's ancestors, but I'm sure that stuff's here, too." Jenna stared out the window, wondering, *If that skeleton dates to the Civil War or the Revolutionary War, everyone I love is innocent.* Jenna smirked at herself and mumbled, "Yeah, right. In a leather jacket and nylon shirt."

"What?"

"Oh, sorry. Just talking to myself. What would you like?"

Aida chose only what her small kitchen would hold.

The next weekend, Marcus left his college in Raleigh and picked up his brother, Anthony, in Chapel Hill, and his brother, Michael, in Durham. They grabbed a quick lunch and drove toward the Blue Ridge mountains. They always used Michael's car because the car the twins shared was too unreliable for the three-hour ride.

As soon as they arrived, the three boys rushed through the front door, calling out, "Mom! We're home!"

Jenna wrapped the skeleton's swatches and cufflink in separate tissue papers and put them in the pocket of her jeans.

The house filled with life, and Jenna imagined Kathleen smiling. Marcus was shorter than his younger brothers but with a more solid build. He had his father's straight black hair and deep brown eyes. Hugging Jenna, he asked, "How are you, Mom? Doing okay?"

Jenna smiled and answered, "I'm fine. I'm just so glad you're all here!"

Michael had Jenna's sable waves and hazel eyes. Just under six feet, he was more reserved and perceptive than his identical twin. Scrutinizing Jenna, he said, "I don't think you can lose Kathleen and be okay."

Anthony had already meandered through the dining room. On the other side, he opened the double doors to the largest room in the house: the library. On the south wall, floor to ceiling bookcases stood sentry between tall windows. On the other windowed wall, a six-foot wide stone fireplace sat between alternating windows and bookcases. Dark oak paneling covered the walls without windows. On the floor, oak planking peeked out from under a faded Turkish area rug.

Crammed into the room were five desks with their chairs, twelve armchairs—most of them mismatched Chippendales—six end tables, and assorted side tables. Every surface held ashtrays, candy dishes, different lamps, and small statues to knock over.

As Jenna and her other sons caught up, Anthony rubbed a window frame and said, "Wow! We spent a lot of summers working on this place." That started her boys swapping stories.

Jenna listened to them reminisce. They had loved Kathleen almost as much as Jenna had but loved the old Victorian more than Jenna did. Jenna's claustrophobia and belief in feng shui had made the overcrowded house as uncomfortable as a rubber Halloween mask.

Marcus, Michael, and Anthony had different reactions to the place. Because Jenna had always saved the royalties from her books for their educations, the four of them had shared a four-room apartment. The boys' three beds had been crammed into what the landlord called a "master" bedroom, while Jenna had squeezed her possessions into a tiny second bedroom. For Jenna's boys, the Victorian and its grounds were better than Disney World.

Jenna never asked Kathleen for financial help, and her friend never offered. They were bound by their laughter and, when necessary, their tears.

Anthony cut through his mother's thoughts with, "Mom?"

Jenna smiled.

He waved his hands in the air and asked, "Where do we start?"

"With dinner."

In the kitchen, the twins set the breakfast bar while Jenna reheated the eggplant parmigiana she had made. Michael mixed chopped olives and artichokes into spring lettuce. "I miss her more in the kitchen," he said with a catch in his throat.

Everyone nodded, and Anthony added,

"You know, Aunt Lia never spent much time here, but when she did come with us, she spent the time wandering the land. It might be why she specializes in environmental law."

Jenna choked on her coffee and thought, *Sweet Jesus! My sister prowled this land.*

"You okay?" Michael asked.

She nodded and refilled Anthony's and Marcus's glasses with chilled tea, then poured Michael's hot tea from a red, iron Chinese pot. Jenna's mind returned to the skeleton, but she slammed those thoughts behind a mental door marked "later" and switched topics. She brought out her lists of chores to do, giving each son a copy. Having grown up with their mother's lists and proofreading her books on organization, they made mock groaning sounds.

"Well," she teased, "I've already done the kitchen and dining room. That's a start."

Marcus raised his eyebrows.

"Okay," she laughed, "I didn't say it was a big start." She refreshed her coffee, and they carried their drinks into the library to plan the next step. Afterward, her boys glanced at the items on the dining room table without wanting anything.

"Sleep," Anthony said. "I only want sleep."

Jenna yawned and admitted, "Me, too. Michael, I put your things from the apartment in the cranberry bedroom on the south corner. Marcus, your stuff is in the green room, so you can watch the sun rise. Anthony, your things are in the gray room. That north corner will keep your paintings cooler. Everything's still boxed, so you can unpack the way you want—"

Anthony interrupted, "Those rooms are so crowded that we won't be able to unpack— or walk. Can our first projects be to clear them out?"

Marcus teased, "I bet Mom has a plan for that too."

Jenna pointed to the lists and said, "Keep the four-poster beds, reduce to one dresser and chest in each bedroom, and store the rest for donation or auction."

On the last word, her stomach lurched, and she closed her eyes. Her forehead beaded with perspiration. When she opened her eyes again, Michael was holding a garbage can under her chin and supporting her.

Jenna grabbed the can and ran through the dining room, across the foyer, and through the sitting room. She made it to the bathroom just in time. After emptying her stomach, she slumped onto the cold, white tile floor. She leaned against the white wainscoting. Her eyes traced the green paint above the wainscoting to the ceiling's white crown molding. Focusing on the molding steadied her.

There was a tap on the door, and Michael asked, "Mom?"

"Need a minute."

"Sick or exhausted?"

Jenna sobbed, "Come in."

Marcus and Michael entered, and she continued. "I've been packing up their lives — Kathleen's, Ronan's, Finn's, and Liam's — as though they meant nothing. I've been donating and selling the last remnants of them as though they weren't my best friends."

"Mom," Marcus said. "Kathleen was incapable of getting rid of anything, but she knew you could."

Jenna did not trust herself to speak.

Michael hesitated and then asked, "Are you okay to sleep in Kathleen's bedroom?"

Jenna found her voice. "Yes," she said, "because your Aunt Lia whirling-dervished it yesterday! She cleared out everything but the canopy bed and dresser." The exhausted woman smiled at the memory and added, "She raided other rooms for tables and lamps — grumbling the whole time, 'Nothing in this house matches!' She ended up settling for anything with an ivory color."

Anthony interjected, "And you replaced Kathleen's heavy drapes with new lace curtains."

"Your aunt bought them, along with new sheets. I almost had to arm wrestle her to keep the bedspread Kathleen quilted — the one with the 'fancy' ivory on ivory stitching. Your aunt did an awful imitation of Kathleen's brogue, saying, 'This sickly smell has to go, don't-cha-know!'"

"At least you're laughing."

"Your aunt made the room mine."

Anthony leaned in and said, "Someone

called. Her name's Carol Ann, and she said you're friends."

Jenna pitched over the toilet and retched again.

Anthony shrugged and said, "I'll tell her you're unavailable."

A few minutes later, all three boys escorted Jenna upstairs. They waited on the landing for her to change into her nightgown and then tucked her into bed as though their roles had reversed.

As they turned off the lamps and closed her door, Marcus insisted, "Sleep."

But sleep did not come. Like a punch in the stomach, she thought about her boys finding the skeleton. That started her wondering if Finn or Liam had found the skeleton, or worse, put the body there. *Would they do that to their mother?* "No," she answered herself. It had been a long tradition in the MacKenna family that boys go back to Ireland to find their wives and bring them to the States. Wives with Irish accents and customs taught their children to speak with brogues and see through life's "blarney." Kathleen's boys had loved their robust and fiery mother too much to do this.

If, by some logic-defying twist, Finn or Liam had a body to bury, neither would have buried it on their mother's land: land that, had they lived, they would have inherited and left to their children. Jenna's thoughts spun in circles until exhaustion won, and she drifted into unstoppable nightmares.

CHAPTER 3
PROGRESS

The next day, as soon as her sons left to run errands, Jenna ran upstairs and changed into jeans and a long-sleeved shirt. She shoved into a cloth shopping bag the drawings she had printed. On the back porch, she opened the large plastic chest where Kathleen kept her painting and garden tools. The chest also contained an assortment of homemade insect repellents and sprays. Jenna rubbed the one for mosquitos on her exposed skin. Then she dropped a selection of tools and a small tarp into the bag. When she had all she thought she needed, she trekked out to the body.

Near the skeleton, she smoothed the

folded tarp into a two-foot by three-foot rectangle. She had watched archeology videos online but gasped, "Oh Lord! I have no idea what I'm doing." She stared through the green canopy at the blue sky and said, "Kathleen, you better be listening because I need you in this mess with me!"

Shaking off her anxiety, Jenna drew the tote closer to herself and pulled out a hand shovel and work gloves. Trembling, she moved thin layers of earth from where she guessed the face might be. She stopped to remove a squiggly worm and lay it a foot away. When her shovel bumped something solid, a jolt of nausea pitched her away from the body.

She groaned and forced herself upright. "This is ridiculous," she moaned. "I've scrubbed toilet bowls, changed diapers, mopped up after vomiting kids, carved turkeys, cleaned out chicken guts, and made liver pate! These are just bare BONES!" She shivered, and a voice inside her head shouted, *But it's a crime: my crime this time.*

Breathing deep, she crawled forward to study the object her shovel had hit. It wasn't bone; it was a tangle of tree roots. Jenna was tempted to cut through them, but she worried she might damage trees and the ensnared skeleton. She stopped. It was still a crime scene, and she did not want to add new damage.

Jenna sat back and said, "Wow, I can't claim ignorance of the law." She winced and added, "But insanity might not be a stretch." Struggling to remain calm, she pulled a wide, soft-tipped paint brush from the tote and shifted soil away from the roots and onto a dustpan. With great care, she shimmied the dustpan to spread the soil on the tarp. A little at a time, she exposed the face below the roots.

Trying to be clinical rather than emotional, she compared the skull with the sketches she had photocopied. The smaller, crowded teeth; the high, narrow nasal passages; and the circular eye sockets with squared margins all resembled the features on the drawing of a male Caucasian skull. She used the brush to clean an indented area above the right eye. When she revealed a jagged crack with a piece out, she said. "Wow, someone hit you hard!"

She thought, *Maybe it was an accident —*

but why would anyone bury an accident victim? With shaking hands, she used the soil she had saved on the canvas to rebury the face. To camouflage the disturbed ground, she spread leaves and broken branches over the entire area. Then, throwing her notes and equipment into her bag, she ran back to the house.

Jenna didn't stop trembling until the equipment was cleaned and back in the tool chest, the cloth shopping bag was in the washing machine with her clothing, and the shredded photocopies of the skulls were under coffee grinds and food scraps in the garbage.

She ran a shower as hot as she could tolerate. Halfway through shampooing her hair, she cried, "Shit!" *I was right there. I should have searched him for his wallet.* Her mind filled with images of the tangled roots from surrounding trees and shrubs. She shook her head and thought, *I would have had to do too much damage to get it out.* After the shower that alternated between hot and cold, Jenna wrapped herself in a robe and moved the quilted bedspread to nap under just a sheet.

It was a relief to have several more

days without an opportunity to go back to the grave. She was grateful for the moans and groans coming from her sons as they made the bedrooms their own. Keeping the original wall color in each bedroom, they followed the strategy of emptying the rooms and returning only what they needed.

During the process, Michael asked, "Mom, have you been able to write at all? I heard you on the phone telling your publisher you need more time."

"It's okay. I'll get to it. But we need to do the sitting room next. Then we'll call Aida and Aunt Lia too, this time."

"Before you do that, Mom. I found a cabin by a lake in the woods. I followed one dirt road then another, most of them dead ends, and finally found Kathleen's cabin — the one where you and Miss Kathleen used to take my brothers and me target shooting. Mom, can I clean and fix it?"

"There's only one cabin, Marcus, but there's three of you."

Anthony chimed in, "There's almost a thousand acres here with other ponds and streams. Michael and I will find other spots for ourselves."

"Actually," Michael said, "After graduation, I want to live in a city and manage a restaurant." He smiled and added, "Mediterranean, with the sauce called 'gravy' and cooked enough for Mom."

"Okay then," Jenna laughed, "the cabin belongs to Marcus. Pick out the furniture you want before I call Aida and Aunt Lia."

After Marcus, then Aida and Lia chose the pieces they wanted, Jenna called the antique dealers and the church consignment shop. After them, she called the auctioneer to take what was left.

The separate bank account Jenna had set up for the proceeds from selling furniture and artifacts grew by the hundreds, then the thousands. It paid for new mattresses and bedding and semi-sheer curtains to replace the heavy, musty draperies. The streaming sunlight sent Anthony running to cover favorite pieces of art until he could move them to dark corners.

Jenna often slipped away to continue her examination of the cufflink. Online, she found a 1980 French coin with the right design. Then she searched for jewelers or dealers who might have sold it as a cufflink. Without Jenna having the authority to request their records, most of the shopkeepers refused to help her. Next, she went through Kathleen's family albums for someone who wore a leather jacket with a dress shirt, but the men in the albums wore suits. The ones who were casual were inside without their jackets.

One day, she snuck away after a hard rain to check on the skeleton. Worried, she used large rocks to create a supporting wall inside the bank near the corpse. Almost done, she stopped and asked herself, "Am I saving the evidence or destroying more of it?" Afterward, in the shower, she moaned, "Oh shit. Why didn't I let the bank collapse and the stream take the damn thing?" The answer came fast. *Because it would hang up somewhere, be found, and might be traced back to Kathleen or her boys.*

Each time her sister visited, Jenna wanted to ask for her help. Lia was a legal pit bull when it came to protecting Mother Nature. She might see something Jenna was missing — something to help solve the mystery. Not wanting to make her sister an accomplice, Jenna remained silent.

Several days later, Marcus said, "That's it. Let's all go out to supper!"

No one argued when Jenna called and invited Aida to join them.

"Yes! Yes, I'd love it."

"I miss Kathleen, too, Aida—and you."

"Thank you, Miss…Jenna."

With Marcus driving and Jenna in the front passenger seat, they pulled up to Aida's apartment. Slim and graceful as a ballerina, the young woman waited outside.

Michael stared out the window and said, "I never noticed how pretty she is. She reminds me of a statue I've seen of Nefertiti."

His twin nudged him and agreed, "Uh huh."

Jenna resisted the urge to glance at Michael. Instead, as Aida slipped into the back seat next to Anthony, Jenna smiled a welcome.

Throughout supper, Michael was almost silent, but Anthony only stopped talking when Marcus cut him off to chat with Aida about her apartment and her job. As Aida chatted and laughed, Jenna's mind wandered back to the day she met her.

***

It had been eight years earlier when Jenna and Kathleen had stopped at the church to see Father Kelly. Startled by a movement in the shadows, Jenna stepped in front of the taller Kathleen. "It" was an undernourished girl with matted hair, filthy clothing, and her thin arms bruised. She also had a blackened eye and split lip. She gripped the front of her blouse to hold it closed. Jenna could not tell her age.

Kathleen had stepped around Jenna to see the child, who had crumpled to the floor. "Oh, Little One," Kathleen cried, "may the devil clean Hell's toilets with the *bodach* who hurt you."

Behind them, Father Kelly gasped, "Kathleen! By the saints, what are you sayin'?"

Kathleen glared at him, red faced, and snapped, "Every saint in Heaven was passed out drunk when the people who hurt this girl and killed my family were born." Then, she turned to the child and said, "Give me your name, and if your family can't be found, you can come work for lodging in my house."

The child had raised her face and whispered, "Aida, ma'am. My name is Aida, and I have no family. I ran away from the orphanage."

***

Jenna came back to the present, wondering, *Might the skeleton be the brute who hurt Aida, or whoever ran Kathleen's family off the road?*

Jenna reminded her sons, "Aida and I have to work tomorrow, but this was fun."

Aida sighed and said, "I do have to call it a night."

They dropped Aida off and went home. After her sons went to bed, Jenna pulled a box from her night table. The fabric swatches and cufflink rested on the cotton inside. She pulled over her laptop to do more research but changed her mind. Tired, she put the little box away and slept.

The next night, she and her sons emptied the sitting room and brought back into it the few pieces they wanted to keep. The day after, Jenna returned from work and went straight into the Victorian's library. She paused to inhale the clean air coming from the open windows and to enjoy floor space and uncluttered tables. In each corner, facing outward, the boys had arranged one desk and chair. A leather couch with comfortable depressions faced the white marble fireplace. For the middle of the room, her sons had chosen Chippendale armchairs, ottomans, end tables, and reading lamps to make a conversation circle.

Jenna went to the desk with her laptop on it. There, she found Post-its from each boy with the reason for his being late. Thinking about the other work that needed to be done, she sighed and thought, *They've earned more than one night off.*

With time alone, she thought more about the cufflinks. They were made from 1980 French coins that any jeweler in the world might have used. *The cufflink might be a dead end,* she thought, *but I wonder if I can find the jacket in a photo.* She lit a fire in the fireplace and curled up on the couch with two more of Kathleen's family albums. Almost as soon as she covered herself with the throw from the back of the couch, her eyes closed.

Two hours later, Michael's voice woke her. "Mom," he whispered, "it's late. Do you want to go upstairs?"

She shivered and mumbled, "Great idea." They climbed the stairway that was wider at the base than where it curved to the second floor. Then, she asked, "Are your brothers home?"

"Not yet. I was with Aida, moving furniture around. She sold four pieces to buy one. Too many flowered prints for me, but she's excited." Michael laughed and added, "Oh, my brothers. I have no idea where they went. Sorry."

Jenna flinched at the thought that her boys might have found the skeleton. *No,* she thought, *that hasn't happened: but it could.* Forcing her thoughts away from her fears, she said, "Michael, I'm not sure Anthony's sensible about women."

Not laughing, Michael answered, "He knows I like Aida, and I trust him. Anyway, I was already with her."

"I wasn't only talking about Aida. Well, he's your twin, but I think you're a decade older."

Michael kissed her forehead before leaving to go to his room.

After she snuggled under the covers, Jenna thought about Aida. She was intelligent, beautiful, and sweet-natured. A girl like that might unintentionally make trouble between brothers. That thought led to bad dreams about her three boys fighting over the skeleton, pulling on its legs and arms until it shattered. Jenna bolted out of her sleep into sunlight. Trembling, she told herself, *I have to trust my boys*. A familiar warmth flowed through her. Her sons had earned her love and trust. They had also proven, beyond doubt, their love for each other.

Breathing easier, she showered and slipped into a summer shift. She placed the box with the cufflink and fabric in her bag. On her way downstairs, the phone rang. She answered the call in the sitting room and inhaled the clean, open space.

The walls were the color of a cloudless twilight sky. Two powder blue Chippendales and a blue and white striped loveseat arced around the birch coffee table in front of the marble fireplace. Tall plants softened the corners of the room. Jenna sunk into one of the armchairs.

The moment she heard Lia's voice, she visualized her sister's arched brows, gray eyes, and unruly brown curls.

Lia started, "How're you doing?"

Jenna's tears flowed as she asked, "Truth?"

"Of course."

Thinking of the skeleton, she said, "I keep expecting to see ghosts."

Lia's voice rose two octaves as she insisted, "We have to get you out of there for a day. Let me think about it. Something Gabe can do with us and your boys — heaven knows, my husband can't male-bond with them over the renovations."

Jenna imagined Gabe in his Brooks Brothers suit with his manicured nails. He was much better at handling power brokers than power tools. "Agreed!" she said. "Call me when you think of something."

Michael appeared in the doorway.

"Coffee's ready," he announced.

Jenna ended the call and followed him into the kitchen. They all made quick work of the coffee and muffins, then Anthony said, "We're doing the basement today, but it's better if we do it without you."

"Why?"

Marcus frowned and said, "It's our rite of passage. When we were young, Miss Kathleen scared us away from there, saying, 'Tis filled to its crumblin' rafters with grumblin' ghosts, don't-cha know. 'Tis not worth your life ta-see it!'"

Michael laughed and admitted, "I believed her when I was little, and still do."

"But," Anthony interrupted, "there might be treasures worth keeping."

With a vigorous shake of his head, Marcus protested, "No second guessing! We drag out what we can burn, scrap metal whatever the junk yard will take, and auction the rest."

Michael asked, "Mom? What do you want us to do?"

"Follow Marcus's lead," she said, "because we already have enough in the house, and we could use more money for repairs." Then, thinking about the mystery, she added, "But set aside books, journals, and paperwork for me. We still have the attic and garages to do, so we'll bring back the dealers and the auctioneer after we finish clearing out every area."

Michael laughed, but insisted, "You go research your next book or write something. We're on a roll."

Her answer was a shaky, "Okay, thanks." Withholding that she intended to search town archives for the names of missing people gave her a stomachache. From their cradles, she had always tried to be honest with them. She even told them that Santa was the "spirit" of giving and that the Easter Bunny was a "reminder" of the Lord's resurrection. No mean kid ever shocked them by shattering myths. Yet it would shock them when she was arrested for however many laws she was breaking.

That night, she returned home without a name for the skeleton. Every night that week, she came back from the office to find the boys filthy, frustrated, and still working in the basement's maze of supporting walls and posts. Instead of slowing them down with her opinions and suggestions, she made them supper and stayed out of their way. Friday night, Jenna came home to find a small U-Haul filled with the metal parts her boys wanted to sell to the scrap yard. She also found her sons inebriated around a giant bonfire. Pretending she was not their mother, she waved at them and went into the basement through the open storm doors.

Gone were the cobwebs and decades of gunk. Her sons had also taken area rugs that had been rolled in corners and spread them over the cement floors to create designated hobby areas. There was an area near windows with Anthony's canvasses and paints and an area for Jenna's sewing equipment. Ronan had taught his boys to build and to repair, and Kathleen had kept all their supplies, so Jenna's sons were able to set up a woodworking space and a corner with scrap metal and welding equipment.

Jenna emerged from the basement and walked to the bonfire saying, "Wow! You shampooed the rugs. I'm impressed."

Anthony slurred, "If we didn't shampoo them, you'd make us go back down and do it."

Michael added, "And, we don't want to see that place again for at least a month."

Smiling, Jenna walked to each boy, kissed him on the head, and stuck out her hand. "Car keys," she said.

Marcus and Michael complied. Anthony stared at her through bleary eyes and hesitated.

"Now," she insisted.

He groaned and handed her his keys.

Jenna kissed the top of his head and smiled. Then she stared at him and said, "If you wake up tomorrow afternoon and think you're sober, you're not. Stay home."

Saturday morning, after Jenna cleaned the dirty bathrooms, she went to the kitchen for a cup of coffee. She tried to focus on the book she was writing but found herself planning the next step in the skeleton mystery. *My mother,* she thought, and picked up the phone to call her.

Alissia and her twin had moved to the southwest for their health. Jenna did not want to discuss the house or inheritance because her mother had always been a little insecure about Jenna's friendship with Kathleen.

"Jenna? What's wrong?"

"Nothing."

"Your sister okay?"

"Yes, she's fine. Something came up in my research, and I was wondering if you remember any missing persons mysteries from when you were young."

"Missing persons? You write books on organization. What does — ?"

Uncomfortable with a lie, she said, "My research can take me in unexpected directions." An image of the skeleton filled her vision, and she choked on her coffee.

"Jenna?"

"I'm okay. My coffee went down the wrong way. So, did anyone go missing when you were younger?"

"No. Grady left, but knowing Belle, the only mystery is that he didn't leave sooner. So, changing the subject, what's happening with the house?"

"I hired an electrician from my office

building to work with Marcus, Michael, and Anthony on the rewiring. I told him my boys know every nail and beam in the house."

"I worry about the work and expenses there."

"We're doing fine on both. My boys are taking the lead on most of it—making it their home now." Having run out of small talk, Jenna made excuses to go and hung up. To herself, she said, *Grady, maybe you didn't leave?*

That night Jenna told her sons about the electrician.

"You know," Anthony said, "Miss Kathleen kept us out of the attic by saying there were big vampire bats up there."

Michael groaned. "And she said the garage was haunted by 'feargach' ghosts!"

"Mom," Marcus laughed, "we grew up believing Miss Kathleen's spooky stories and stayed out of those places—even after we didn't believe the stories anymore."

"Who didn't believe them anymore?" Anthony yelled. "Didn't you hear all the moaning and groaning while we worked in the basement?"

Michael teased, "Yeah. Most of it came from you."

Everyone laughed except Jenna, who was thinking about Kathleen's ghost stories, card readings, and seances. All they had done for Jenna was prove that she did not have a psychic bone in her body. Still, a few of Kathleen's stories may have been meant to keep the boys away from "eight generations of precarious pilings," while others may have kept her sons away from clues: clues they had now, inadvertently, cleared away.

Later that night, after her sons went to bed, Jenna paused on the large second-floor landing. Between two of the bedroom doors, a well-padded tan club chair, next to a small table with a tall lamp, waited for an occupant. She was tempted to sit, but curio cabinets in two of the landing's corners called to her. One held a collection of jade and the ivory items scavenged from other rooms. "Wow," Jenna said aloud. *Oh Kathleen, with everything such a jumble, I never appreciated how beautiful the individual pieces are!* Anticipating more treasures, Jenna moved over to the other curio, and a sob escaped her body. Matchbox cars and plastic cowboys and horses filled all four shelves. *Finn and Liam's toys!* Jenna did not know where her sons found them, but they had cleaned and arranged them with great care.

Afraid she might cry out and wake her boys, Jenna rushed down to the library. There, she curled into a corner of the leather couch and forced herself to focus on the mystery. *Was the guy's disappearance explained at the time — like with Grady's leaving?* A notable percentage of Jenna's classmates had gone away to college and never returned. Others relocated for jobs. Of course, if the missing man was Kathleen's schoolmate, Jenna would not have known him. *I need to go to the police*, she thought, *because they have forensics and can solve this.* To herself, she said, "Oh God! They still might suspect Kathleen, Ronan, or their sons."

Jenna never had a lot of friends. The few she had were priceless: Finn, Liam, Gabe, and Carol Ann — Grady and Belle's daughter, who broke off their friendship in high school. All those years before, at the funeral for Ronan, Finn, and Liam, Carol Ann stood on one side of the caskets with her boyfriend, Billy. Jenna stood on the other side of the caskets with Finn and Liam's teammate, Christian.

Carol Ann and Jenna's mothers comforted Kathleen. Belle, inappropriate as usual, had belittled her daughter with the snide remark, "Nice of my Carol Ann to scrap her manners and bring a date."

During the committal, Christian had touched Jenna's hand and then held it. As the caskets lowered, he placed a supporting arm around her. Jenna felt him trembling through his varsity jacket.

A week later, Carol Ann married Billy, and they had Callie a few months after that. Jenna spent her college years studying and healing with Christian and Kathleen, who started to smile again.

After college, Jenna and Christian married, but the two hot-tempered alphas divorced when their twins were five. "'Tis a blessing," Kathleen used to tell Jenna, "that Christian's a good daddy and your boys can visit him often." Then she would glare in the direction of the cemetery, and add, "Not all of

God's plans are shyte."

Shaking off the past, Jenna stared into the unlit fireplace and mused, *I might be going about this all wrong. Right now, I need sleep.* Standing to leave the room, she glanced at the bookshelves that held Kathleen's family albums. There were no photos between the deaths of Kathleen's sons and the births of Jenna's. Then she noticed the stack of papers and journals her boys had brought from the basement. She told herself, *I don't have the energy for them right now.* Trying to rub the sticky dust off her hands, she climbed the stairs to her bathroom.

CHAPTER 4
THE ABBOTT CLAN

The next morning, she discussed with her sons the need to clean out the attic, and later that day, Jenna returned from her job to clean up a dust trail through the house.

That Saturday morning, Lia called. "Jenna," she said in her no-nonsense, lawyer's voice. "Your sons need a break, and so do you. I've prepared a picnic basket with fried chicken, cold salads, and sweet tea. Don't say no to the 4th of July picnic in the park outside of town."

Instead of saying no, Jenna said, "I look forward to it!"

A few hours later, she found herself

helping her sister spread the tablecloth and set out the food. The boys ate as though it were a race, then dispersed while Jenna, Lia, and Gabe ate slower. Afterward, Jenna stretched out on her blanket, appreciating gentle breezes and the bird calls in nearby trees. Her reveries were shattered by a soprano voice. She bolted upright.

"Jenna!" called Carol Ann. "Jenna!" The reed-thin woman with heavy makeup baking in the heat waved as she approached. Plopping down on Jenna's blanket, she exclaimed, "My! You haven't changed since high school. You're still an adorable pixie!"

And, Jenna thought, *if you remember anything about me, you know I hate being called adorable.* "With fifteen more pounds and crow's feet," Jenna corrected her.

"You were always much too thin, but you're fine now."

Before Jenna thought of a response, another overly enthusiastic blast from the past called to her. "Hi, cutie!"

Jenna almost upchucked her lunch but swallowed hard and answered, "Hi, Billy."

As he squatted on her blanked, uninvited and with his legs wide open in front of her, Jenna searched for something polite to say. He was paunchy, but—judging from his arms—not soft, so she observed, "You look like you still work out."

The man beamed, rubbed his slight roundness, and said, "Racquetball, jogging, weights...once a jock, always a jock."

Jenna nodded, wondering if he realized that "jock" was not always a compliment.

Carol Ann said, "Well, people want to buy from the ones with grain in their silos and a belt goin' through every loop. Even the customer who carries a Medicare card in her mini-skirt pocket wants a realtor who knows better."

Jenna suppressed a groan.

"Speaking of our business...," Billy began.

"Mom!"

Despite the voice being female, Jenna turned with Carol Ann.

The young woman rushing toward them was all blonde curls and a pout. She had a toddler in tow. Jenna disliked the forceful way the young woman dragged the boy and the whiney way she said, "Mom. Have y'all seen Clay?"

It was Carol Ann's turn to frown. "Callie," she reprimanded, "we're talking business."

"Actually," Jenna interrupted, "I need to find my sister. Why don't you help Callie find her husband, and we'll catch up later?" Not waiting for anyone to delay her, Jenna hurried away. She glanced over her shoulder only long enough to see Carol Ann and Billy arguing with each other and ignoring Callie's distress. Jenna faced forward just before crashing into her brother-in-law. "Gabe," she gasped, "thank God it's you."

Gabe peered at her and said, "What's going on? I don't like how pale you are, and you're shaking!" He led her over to a big oak tree and ordered, "Sit before you fall."

Grateful for the solid earth beneath her, Jenna declared, "I was just fleeing the Abbotts."

"Ah," he sympathized. "They must want you to sell."

"Will you go over my finances with me?

You and my boys, because I'm not sure which one will end up executor."

"Whoa! Are you planning your funeral already?"

"I'm surrounded by death."

"Besides Kathleen, who?"

Stunned for a moment, she squashed a memory of the body and said, "Sorry. I'm just a little overwhelmed."

"I'm not sure that house and its memories are good for you. But since I'm not going away again until mid-July, we can get together any night this week."

"Tuesday?"

"I'll be at your house at seven."

Jenna breathed easier and smiled. A familiar shape emerging from the crowd caught her eye. She waved and called out, "Hey, Sis!"

Lia had just sat next to Jenna when a grating voice called to them. "Hello, y'all! You found a wonderful spot!" It was Carol Ann again. Sunlight made her blonde hair glow. Holding Callie's little boy as though he were dirty laundry, she rushed over and dropped onto the grass beside Jenna. After plopping the child alongside herself, she said, "Have y'all met my grandson? Hard to believe I'm a grandmother. I mean, I'm only a year younger than you, and your boys are still in college. Oh, and Marcus! If your oldest didn't have a big home to come back to, he might move on with his life."

Not wanting to keep the focus on Marcus, Jenna bit back a reaction.

Lia and Gabe remained silent as well.

"Of course," Carol Ann rambled on, "I only beat you to it, Jenna, because sons don't get married as early as daughters." Then, with an edge on each word, she announced, "Anyway, this is Josh. He's two."

Josh pulled a fistful of grass.

Carol Ann groaned. "My daughter is searching everywhere for that husband of hers. I swear, she couldn't find up or down in an elevator." Flashing a quick smile, she continued with, "Well, don't the women in this town just have more trouble with their men?" Then she wagged a finger and insisted, "Think about it. Kathleen's husband and sons are gone—not that they left on purpose. Then,

Jenna, your husband left. My son-in-law's God knows where. My husband — well, bless him — he's got what it takes to take what you've got, doesn't he?" She blushed, stammered, and dove back in with, "I swear, Lia's got the best man in town!" She stared at Gabe as though he were steak on a plate.

Gabe shifted his feet.

Lia's eyes blazed, but she smiled and agreed, "He's a keeper."

"Well, they do say the road to Hell is paved with good intentions."

"It's paved with husband-stealers, too," Lia sniped.

Gabe choked on nothing, and Lia stood to rub his back until he breathed again.

Jenna changed the subject with, "Carol Ann, I think Callie's as pretty as can be."

"Well," Carol Ann snorted, "her marrying Clay Corbell was like fishin' on a dock over sand! Of course, if either of your twins had paid her any attention first, Josh might have been your grandson, too." She stroked the boy's head as though it was required.

"He's beautiful," Jenna said.

The boy gave her a bright smile, and Jenna wondered how much time the family needed to dim his lights.

Anthony appeared and sat next to the child. He smiled and asked, "And who are you?"

The child answered. "Josh." He wobbled to his feet and toddled over to plop in the young man's lap. With great care, he placed a fist-full of crumpled grass in Anthony's upturned palm. Anthony crumpled it more and returned it to Josh's palm. Thus, a new game was invented.

While Jenna and the others talked, Anthony and the child were content to keep each other company. The toddler had been babbling for several minutes when he stopped and frowned. The sudden change had everyone staring at him.

Josh's mother came between the small group and the sunlight. She pouted and dropped onto the grass near her son. Josh nestled closer to Anthony.

Lia stood and pulled at her husband and sister but, mindful of Josh, she said, "Come on. Let's find i-c-e c-r-e-a-m."

"Want any?" Jenna asked her son.

He shook his head and answered, "Just had fried rum runners."

"Well, I'm starving," Carol Ann cut in. "So I'll come too."

Jenna glanced at her son with Josh and Callie and registered some discomfort, but her sister pulled her away.

The rest of the day was a blur of people, games, and eating. Callie and Josh stayed with Anthony, while Callie's husband was always elsewhere. Late that afternoon, Jenna said to Lia, "I'm worried that Anthony will feel compelled to rescue Callie."

"Why Callie?"

Jenna frowned and said, "Because she has 'rescue me' tattooed to her forehead. Ugh! I'll have him drive me home, and try to warn him off the girl."

Michael appeared with Aida and stayed only long enough to say, "I'll get him," before leaving again.

A few minutes later, in the car with Anthony, Jenna worried she might be over-reacting about Callie. Deciding not to broach that subject, she said, "I appreciate all the work you and your brothers are doing on the house. This would have been impossible without you."

"You're working, and we're home from college. It's a no-brainer."

She stopped herself at "Thanks."

Without comment, Anthony dropped her off, then peeled out to return to the picnic.

Jenna went straight to the library to examine the papers from the basement. Dusty and yellowed, they turned out to be condolences on the loss of Kathleen's family. There were also unopened cards with the same postal dates. Jenna wept through the reading of every open letter without finding a clue. Then she put all the opened and unopened cards in an envelope labeled "Kathleen" and found a place for it on one of the bookshelves.

After a much-needed shower, she returned to the library with a notepad to work on her next book. Hours later, Jenna woke on the couch with the blank notepad on her lap. Except for nightlights, the quiet house was dark. Upstairs, Jenna peeked into each boy's room the way she had been doing since they were infants. In Michael's room, a nightlight showed a little clutter on the end table and only the clothing from the picnic on the floor. Marcus's room was meticulous. Jenna hesitated in front of Anthony's door. Now that he had a room of his own, he kept it like a Picasso abstract — everything in unexpected places. She braced herself and peeked inside. Moonlight streaked across a tiny person on the bed, surrounded by pillows and rolled blankets.

Stunned for a second, Jenna looked again. The only tiny person she knew at that time did not belong there. Jenna backed out of the room and tiptoed downstairs. On the love seat in the sitting room, Callie lay curled up, asleep, with a throw blanket covering her legs. Anthony was sprawled lopsided in an armchair with one foot on the ottoman and one on the floor.

Puzzled about her new guests, Jenna tiptoed into the kitchen to put on water for herbal tea. She changed her mind and poured Emmet's Irish Cream into a crystal cordial. A movement turned her toward the archway between the kitchen and the entrance foyer.

Callie stood there, rumpled, with a bruised cheek, split lip, and tears in her eyes. "I...I...I'm sorry to intrude, Miss Jenna," she stammered, "but your boys saw me upset and trying to get my screaming baby in my car, and Anthony offered to drive me here."

"You're hurt. Was Josh hurt, too?"

"No. Just scared."

"I have an herbal tea that might help you sleep."

Callie murmured, "Actually, if you don't mind, I'd like some of what you're drinking."

"It might burn that lip."

"But it will be better for my courage than the tea."

Jenna brought out a stemless cocktail glass to pour her guest a little more than she had for herself. "Follow me," she said, and led the injured woman out of the kitchen, through the dining room, and into the library. She turned on two table lamps and gestured toward the three-seat leather couch. Putting her glass on the end table, she lit a small fire in the marble fireplace. It was more for emotional comfort than heat.

"My ma says I've spent my whole life followin' empty wagons waiting for something to fall out. It hurts, you know. It hurts that she's right about me." The girl gazed into the fireplace.

Mean, Jenna thought. *Grandmother to mother, mother to daughter – inherited malice hiding behind southern humor.* "Trying and failing," Jenna whispered. Then she glanced at the young woman, who had fallen asleep. Jenna let the liqueur, silence, and small flames dancing in the deep fireplace quiet her nerves until her eyes began to close.

Callie's attempt to suppress a sob yanked Jenna out of a dream about weeping bones.

Despite the heat, Callie had pulled the throw over herself. "I couldn't go home," she murmured, staring at the darkening bruises on both of her forearms, "because I would have received more of this."

Jenna kept her eyes on the fire.

"I can't go to my parents about Clay. Pa thinks Clay supporting me is the only important thing. My ma's never been…okay – not in my entire memory. Pa says her father walking out 'permanently frayed' her. Miss Jenna, you knew my ma before that happened; did you know my Grandpa Grady, too?"

Before Jenna thought of a response, little Josh let out a wail upstairs.

"Sweet Lord," Callie cried, trying to untangle herself from the throw blanket. "How could I leave my baby in a strange place like that? Ma says I wouldn't get the same number twice if I counted my ears, and she's right!" After freeing her legs, she ran out of the room.

When Callie did not return, Jenna stayed in front of the fire. Thoughts about Carol Ann's father, Grady, triggered memories of him with her father, Matteo, and Kathleen's husband, Ronan. The three men had been best friends since kindergarten. That's why their wives were often together. That's why Jenna and the other children were raised like cousins.

She wondered who the men's other friends were and if one of them had disappeared. She thought about her dad and told him, *Maybe it's a good thing you died eight years before the accident; at least you're in the clear.* Sitting up, she mumbled, "How on earth can I clear Kathleen and her boys?" *Another reason not to turn this over to the police,* she thought, *is that they might think my cleaning out the house was a cover-up.* She groaned and leaned back. *My next book might be titled, Organizing Jail Cells.*

CHAPTER 5
UNLIKELY SOURCES

The next morning, Jenna lurched out of a dream about cleaning a jail cell. Staring around the library, she chuckled at the realization that the cell had belonged to Dale "The Whale" Biederbeck from the TV show, *Monk*. She groaned, "I'm making myself crazy." Then, to do something besides think, she closed the flue and shoveled cold ashes out of the fireplace into the lidded brass bucket. Afterward, she shuffled into the kitchen, where Marcus sat at the breakfast bar. "I'm off work today," she told him.

"The electrician is coming. We'll try not to rip off walls, but we might do some damage."

"Your brothers?"

"Josh woke us early, so Anthony took him and Callie for breakfast. Michael went back to sleep. I'm wondering if we'll have someone else moving in—with a little someone else."

Jenna groaned and said, "If Callie moves in here, Carol Ann will nest on our porch, with Billy and Clay behind her. The only thing worse would be Anthony dropping out of school."

"I'd never quit school," Anthony said from the archway. "Even if Callie and I became more than friends."

"Is she going back to Clay?" Marcus asked.

"No," his brother answered while pouring himself iced tea. "She drove Josh to an aunt's house." Leaning against the counter, he asked, "Mom, what was Carol Ann like in school?"

"Hmm. Well, we were friends in elementary school, but her dad left when we were high school freshmen. After that, Carol Ann changed. She dressed different, acted different, and wanted boys more than she wanted a best friend."

Entering the room, Michael added, "Maybe having a boyfriend made her feel safe."

"Wait here," Jenna said, as though any of them had made a move to leave. She hurried to the library and to the shelf where she had cleared room for her albums. She brought one back from the eighties and opened it on the kitchen counter. She flipped through pages until she came to photos of herself with Carol Ann. "Here we are," Jenna pointed, "with my mom and Carol Ann's mother, Belle. My mother and Kathleen thought Belle drove her husband to drink with all her complaining— but, with their three husbands best friends, we were all drawn together. The day this photo was taken, our parents took us kids for ice cream after church."

She turned a page and said, "This one's a month later. My dad had died of a heart attack a few years before, but Grady and Ronan made sure to include me with their kids. In these next pictures, we're out for burgers with Finn and Liam."

Seeing her friends flooded Jenna with warmth until the image of Grady caught her eye. She stared at the photo and then stared harder. There it was. She had studied the skeleton's swatches for so long that there was no forgetting the colors. Carol Ann's father was wearing the same leather jacket and green shirt as the body on Kathleen's land.

"Mom," Michael said from the doorway, "your hands are shaking. How long ago was this? When were Ronan and his sons killed?"

"The accident was thirty-one years ago."

"I'm sorry it still hits you so hard. I hoped changing the house would help."

"Michael, it does help."

"Well," Marcus interjected, "You think you'll be okay if we move on to the garage?"

Jenna assured them, "Of course, you know I'll be fine."

"Then we'll go on and clear the garage bays. The electrician's coming around three. Can you walk him around?"

Jenna straightened her back, lifted her chin, and said, "Sure! Do what you have to."

After her boys left for the garage, Jenna finished the dishes then rushed to the gravesite. She sat on the ground near the skeleton and stared at where she had hidden the hand under brush. She whispered, "Well, Grady Delford, I guess you didn't abandon Belle and Carol Ann, after all." *I need to tell them that*, she thought. *But not until I'm sure Kathleen didn't put you here.* She calculated that Kathleen was about forty-eight or forty-nine when Grady disappeared. She stared at the mile and a half of forest, roots, and shrubs between the skeleton and the private road to the house. *I don't think she could push a wheelbarrow through the woods. Could she have dragged you in here on a hunter's sled?* Aloud she said, "No! Even if she had the strength, she wouldn't let Carol Ann feel abandoned all these years. Not unless Kathleen thought there was something worse than the girl feeling abandoned."

Sobbing, she murmured, "Oh my God, Grady. Are you the one who ran Kathleen's family off the road that night? Did you kill them?"

"No!" Jenna shouted to no one. Shaking her head, she said, "I don't know." Then she wondered, *If Grady killed his last best friend, wouldn't he have had the conscience to say so? Even with a wife and child to protect?*

If Kathleen killed Grady for killing Ronan and their sons, wouldn't she have had the conscience to confess? Even with an estate to keep out of Belle's litigious and jealous hands? Jenna murmured, "Maybe not."

Back then, Belle and Carol Ann were already complaining about Grady's drinking. *So, he might not have remembered causing the accident.* "What a mess!" Jenna cried out. She stood and brushed leaves and dirt off her pants. Trying not to think about it anymore, she headed back to the house.

She arrived to find the electrician knocking on the door. "Oh!" she said. "I'm sorry. I thought you were coming later."

"A job canceled. Hope you don't mind my showing up early."

Opening the door to let him in, she said, "Of course not. Come in."

"To tell you the truth," the man said, "when I realized y'all were calling me to work on Miss Kathleen's house, I almost said 'no' — but, wow! Y'all worked miracles. I can move around in here to find the problems."

Jenna wasn't sure if Kathleen had been insulted or she was complimented. Choosing the latter, she said, "Thanks. Would you like iced tea?"

Without taking his eyes off the walls, he said, "Yes, thank you."

A few minutes later, she was back with the tray and offered him a glass. As he straightened up from his examination, she asked, "Did you know my father and Grady and Ronan?"

"They were a couple of years ahead of me in school. They were nice enough to us younger kids but stayed together most of the time."

"I think Grady partied harder than my dad and Ronan."

The electrician laughed. "Yes, ma'am! That Grady downed beer by the case, but he was always quiet about it. He didn't turn to the hard stuff until later — after your pa, and Ronan and Ronan's boys were gone." The old man's voice trembled. "I thought losing all of them would kill Grady, too, so I was surprised he lived long enough to run off the way he did. Well, it's done and past, ain't it?" Shaking his head, he moved into the library where, still slender and spry, he knelt to study something behind an armchair. "I'm finding faulty outlets and bad wiring everywhere," he explained. "But your Marcus negotiated a break in the price if your three boys work with me, and I don't have to hire help." He paused, his face flushed, and added, "Well, I don't normally let owners help me, 'cause they usually make my work harder."

"But...."

"But, after talking to them, I decided to take a chance."

"You will find that they never say they can do something if they can't."

"Well, I'll start making a list of the first things we need to fix."

At that point, Jenna realized she could not finesse the conversation back to Grady.

Sitting in bed that night, she reviewed her conversation with the electrician and decided it had not been helpful. Grady's drinking heavier after Kathleen's family was killed made sense, even if he did not run them off the road. *But he wasn't alone*, Jenna thought. *Why didn't having*

Belle and Carol Ann help him through it?

Jenna sat straighter in bed. "That's it!" she said aloud, then thought, *Belle, is the next one to ask — if I can visit her in the nursing home.* Jenna reached for her cell phone and texted her supervisor an apology for the last-minute notice and a request for the next day off.

Her boss texted back, *Of course! Susan can cover. Email her instructions. Hope you're okay.*

Jenna responded, *I'm fine. Thank you. I'll contact her, now.* Then she went to her computer, created an email with a brief list of tasks, and sent it to Susan. She also emailed those students who might be upset about her cancelling their guidance sessions. Going slowly, she proofed each communication three times before sending it.

The next morning, she had breakfast with her sons and appreciated their enthusiasm. The basement had become a workshop for their crafts and hobbies. The attic housed only Christmas and Halloween decorations. Their cars occupied the three garage bays. The house held only treasures. She shared her sons' relief that the major clean-up projects were complete.

"I don't know if Kathleen is smiling or crying," Jenna murmured.

"Smiling," Anthony said, "because we can see the house, really see the house, instead of the stuff in it!"

"Careful," Jenna warned. "Kathleen loved that 'stuff.'"

"But she gave it to you, knowing you wouldn't."

"Anyway," Marcus interrupted, "after the electrician and plumber rip up walls, we'll be in the spackling and painting stage, and it'll be a mess again." Marcus touched her shoulder and said, "Don't worry, Mom. We'll salvage the floorboards and as much of the tiling as we can. I'll check out a few tile places today for matching pieces or design pieces to replace the ones we'll shatter."

Anthony added, "Michael and I will search lumber yards for planks, stains, and varnishes that can help us match the old flooring."

Michael sipped his coffee and smiled. "It'll be fine, Mom," he said. "We won't let Kathleen down."

After breakfast, her sons rushed off. While Jenna cleaned the kitchen, she hoped the receptionist at the front desk would let her in to see Belle.

CHAPTER 6
UNCOMFORTABLE ANSWERS

All the way to the nursing home, Jenna wondered if she should have asked Carol Ann to put her on a visitors' list, but Jenna had no viable excuse to give her former friend. Before opening the door, she breathed deeper. Then, standing at the front desk, she exhaled and waited.

"Jenna?"

Jenna stared at the woman behind the counter and then exclaimed, "Sally!"

"Yes! I've been working here ever since the school laid me off."

"I'm sorry. I only heard about it after you left."

"Everyone else was nice enough to sign the card, but you sent a note asking what you could do to help. That was real special. Anyway, darlin', what can I do for you?"

"I've come to see Belle Delford."

"Oh, that's right," Sally said with a smile. "You and Carol Ann were as close as kin when we were all kids. Let me get a nurse to escort you; this place is such a maze. I keep telling them to paint stripes on the corridor floors that our residents can follow to the cafeteria or the TV room, but bless their hearts if they aren't more willing to let a few old folks get lost each month than to pay for paint." After a moment, she pointed to a heavy, silver-haired nurse. "Betty, please take Miss Jenna to see Belle Delford."

Sally had been right about the corridors' being a maze. Styles and materials changed where wings interlocked, implying little or no attempt at conformity. Twice, the nurse who guided her hesitated at an intersection of hallways. When they arrived at a door with Belle's nameplate on it, the silent nurse nodded and left. Jenna hesitated, then knocked.

A voice rasped, "Well, don't just stand out there. Come and refill my water glass." As Jenna entered, the old woman snapped, "Well, come closer and let me see ya." After Jenna did as she was instructed, the old woman peered at her with eyes the same blue as Carol Ann's. Then she demanded to know, "So? Who are you?"

"Jenna Rossi. I was Jenna Conti when Carol Ann and I were friends."

"Matteo's girl?"

"Matteo and Alissia."

"Your pa was a gorgeous hunk of man, but your ma can't count to twenty with her socks off."

Jenna stiffened at the insult but did not respond.

The woman's bones were visible through dry skin, and her compressed and twisted frame looked painful. "Yes, yes, yes," Belle groused. "Carol Ann always came back dirty from playin' outside with you."

Jenna smiled and admitted, "I played inside for her, and she played outside for me."

"Makes no never mind. She didn't need

to clean up none for the marryin' she did. That girl of mine and her girl too—neither of 'em can tell a skunk from a housecat."

"Belle, Carol Ann stopped our friendship in high school. Do you know why?"

The woman's gray skin tinted pink. "Of course I do! I'd never forget those tragedies! Did you know I had a crush on Ronan?"

Stunned at the disconnected admission, Jenna did not answer.

Belle frowned and continued. "'Course I did. He was my husband's best friend, but he was worth ten of my Grady. Ronan didn't drink. His pay made it to the grocery store. His bills got paid. And, oh Lordy, but his smile made it all the way to his eyes. Kathleen melted every time that man glanced her way, and I can still imagine what went on in that bedroom—"

"Miss Belle," Jenna interrupted a little more forcefully than she intended. Then she repeated, "Do you know why Carol Ann stopped our friendship?"

The old woman's frown deepened, and she spoke without straightening it. "Those were horrible times. Unforgiveable things happened."

"Grady?" Jenna prompted.

"His friends thought he was great fun when he was drinkin'. That's 'cause they weren't moppin' his puke off the bathroom floor. You know, girl, how long a minute is depends upon what side of the outhouse door you're on. Livin' with Grady—especially after that night—was like havin' my head in the hole."

"That night?"

The old woman shouted, "What's wrong with you? Sweet Lord, Alissia, you must have seen that Grady ended his life with Ronan's and Finn's and Liam's!"

Jenna let the old woman think she was her mother.

Belle rambled on, saying, "He couldn't go on from there. We couldn't go on from there." She shivered and spat out the words, "It's a good thing there's more than one use for a frying pan." Then her eyes lost focus, and spittle dripped from one side of her mouth.

Jenna hit the emergency button for the nurse. While she waited for help, she used a tissue to dab away the drool. Afraid she might tear the fragile skin, Jenna backed away. With a shaking hand, she threw the tissue in the trash. Biting her lip and crossing and uncrossing her arms, she paced while waiting for Betty. *Did I do this?* she wondered. *Did I give Belle a stroke?*

Betty checked Belle's pulse and her eyes. "She's all right, ma'am," she said to Jenna. "Belle gets this way; she just drifts off." Betty adjusted the white blanket on Belle's lap, bringing it a little higher to cover the old woman's sunken chest, and said, "You come with me, now, and let her rest. I'll send someone back to put her to bed, but please visit again. She drives away the staff, so they rush through what they need to do and leave. Heaven knows, Miss Belle's daughter can't stay much past hello." Leading Jenna down the hallway, the woman added, "Belle's all spit and jagged glass, but no one should live their last years alone. Maybe you'll find your way back."

Saying "Maybe," Jenna thought, *Hell no*. Belle, Kathleen, and Alissia had been thrown together by their husbands' unbreakable bonds. The tensions between the three women were like static electricity, making the hair rise of the necks of their children. Jenna came away from the nursing home with a better understanding of that friction and realizing that she had one more person to question.

At home, she climbed the stairs to the second-floor landing, sunk into the old club chair, and called her mother on the landline.

"Jenna? Is something wrong? You sound tired."

"Everything's okay, Mom. My boys are fine, but I've been missing Dad and Kathleen's family."

"It comes and goes, doesn't it, sweetheart? The missing them, I mean. Did something trigger it?"

"I saw Carol Ann at the Fourth of July picnic and started wondering about the tensions between Belle and you and Kathleen. I noticed it when I was too young to understand."

There was a long silence before her mother's voice tightened, and she asked, "Does it matter, now?"

"Yes. Dad, Grady, Ronan, Kathleen's sons, and the three of you — it's all one puzzle that's keeping me awake."

"Let me pour myself another cup of coffee."

In the minute her mother was gone, Jenna tried not to think.

"All right then," her mother said in a tense voice. "I have a confession. After Kathleen's husband and sons died, I was jealous of how close you and she became. I was proud of you for helping her through that nightmare, but I'm embarrassed to say I thought I was losing you to her."

A fist hit Jenna in the middle of her chest, and she murmured, "I'm sorry, Mom."

"It's all right, honey, I know I didn't lose you, and I'm grateful that Kathleen has given you and your boys more than I've ever had — but not if the inheritance is hurting you."

"The only thing bothering me is unanswered questions. Like, what about Belle?"

"Well, our family migrated from the northeast, and Kathleen was from Ireland. It was Belle — before she married Grady — who was a sweet, young, southern charmer. Only after she married Grady did she become dissatisfied with what she called 'my white trash' life."

Alissia paused, sipped her coffee, and then added, "I think it was jealousy. Ronan brought Kathleen home, and, as the only boy, he inherited the estate. It turned Belle bright green. The more Kathleen and I loved our husbands and children, the more dissatisfied Belle became with Grady and poor Carol Ann. Kathleen said to me once, 'I do believe that woman could kill me in my sleep to take my home and family.'"

"What did you say to that?"

"I said, 'Even Belle must know that Ronan would never love anyone but you.' Well, Kathleen just smiled. She was so beautiful, Jenna. She had red hair, green eyes, fair skin, and just a few freckles. She was tall and slim, too. I was shorter with curves that made me dumpy later. I loved her like a sister, but I never felt pretty next to her."

Jenna scolded, "Mom! Dad always compared you to Gina Lollobrigida!"

Her mother said, "I remember," and

laughed.

The deep, rich sound of it brought back Jenna's memory of her parents hugging and whispering on their front porch swing. Jenna softened her voice and said, "I have your eyes, and despite my keeping it short, I have your thick, wavy hair—and your curves. Should I be unhappy about how I look?"

"Point well taken," her mother sighed.

"Do you think Belle really wanted Ronan?"

Alissia paused before saying, "Belle wanted everything Kathleen had—most of all, Ronan. Ronan's accident devasted Kathleen, but it was Grady who drank harder and Belle who became hateful."

"When I was still friends with Carol Ann, her mother was terrible to her and her dad."

"Kathleen used to say—," Alissia came closer to Kathleen's brogue than anyone else. "'Even the devil won't go near that house.' And she believed it. Still, we should have done more to help Grady and his daughter. I don't know what, but something."

"Thank you, Mom," Jenna said. "You

helped make sense of my memories."

"You're welcome. You're sure you're okay?"

"I'm fine. We're all tired, but your grandsons have done an incredible job with the place."

"They have always loved it. Kathleen told me once, 'It's a grand thing Jenna and the boys will be doin.' They'll keep what needs keepin' and lose what needs losin.'"

Thinking about the body, Jenna stammered, "She said that?"

"Kathleen made me promise not to tell you about the will, in case she had nothing left to leave you. She was tired, Jenna. The last time we talked, she said, 'I'm knackered, Alissia, and my men are holdin' a seat for me in Heaven.'"

"Thank you for telling me."

"I love you, honey, but your aunt is waiting for us to leave for canasta night. Give your sister my love."

Jenna said, "I will! Have fun." Then she decided to postpone thinking about what her mother had said until later. Instead, she went down to the kitchen to start supper.

CHAPTER 7
CABIN FEVER

The next day, after work, Jenna pulled in front of her house to find a dark blue pickup truck parked there: Clay's. Her first instinct was to stay in her car.

Clay staggered around from the driver's side of his vehicle. He was a little under six feet with a head-start on a beer belly. He would have been handsome without the red blotches from alcohol abuse. "I want my damn wife!" he shouted.

Endangered, Jenna pulled her gun from the glove compartment. She stood between the car door and its frame, keeping the gun out of sight. "Hello to you too, Clay."

"Where's Callie?"

"I just came home. Michael's shopping with Aida. Anthony and Marcus are searching for new floorboards — "

"I don't give a damn about none of that."

"It means there wasn't anyone here to let Callie inside. So, goodbye and have a nice day somewhere else."

"B-b-bitch!" he screamed, stumbling toward her.

"Well, now, you have to hope this is my bitchy side because my scared side is crazier."

"I-I-I've got a shotgun in the car, and I-I-I can b-b-blow your scrawny ass off!"

Jenna raised her gun and said, "Your shotgun's in your truck, and my 'scrawny ass' already has her gun. Be smart and go home."

"I'll ki — "

"Stop! That's not smart."

Slamming his fist on the hood of his truck, he shouted, "I hate b-b-back-talkin' women."

"On your way home, why don't you stop for four or five or six more beers? You've earned them."

"Six?"

"Sure! You're man enough."

He nodded and stumbled back to his truck, yelling, "Damn straight."

As she watched the truck skid on the gravel trying to aim for her private road, she put her gun back into the glove compartment and called 911. A familiar and welcomed voice answered, "Sergeant Harley here."

"Sergeant, this is Jenna Rossi, from our chess club. Clay Corbell was just here, and he's hammered."

"I'm not surprised, Miss Jenna."

"He may be headed for the first bar between my house and his."

"We'll get him, but if he's drunk, you should have kept him there."

"Sergeant, have I or any of my sons ever been in your jail?"

"No, ma'am."

"Well, let's keep it that way."

He laughed and said, "Yes, ma'am."

After hanging up, Jenna slipped behind the wheel, locked her gun in the glove compartment, and drove around the house to the garages. The day before, Marcus, Michael, and Anthony had installed door openers and given her the controls for the first bay. As the door rose, she saw legs. The door continued to rise and revealed Callie with her right arm in a sling and her left hand holding little Josh's. Between them, a diaper bag sat on the floor. As the car pulled in, Callie shuffled the bag with her feet while she led Josh to the side.

Jenna stepped out of the car and stared at the girl, trying to figure out what was wrong with her face. Coming closer, she saw that a second split on Callie's lip was stitched, one eye was blackened, and the whole left side of her face was swollen. Jenna swallowed hard to hold back tears.

"The bay doors wouldn't raise for me," the young woman explained, "but the side door was unlocked. I'm sorry if I'm bringing y'all trouble, but I need a place to hide Josh."

"I thought you were at your cousin's."

"Ma told Pa that I was there. He told Clay where I was, so Clay found me and did this. He would have done worse if my cousin's husband hadn't pulled him off."

Jenna froze, frowning.

"My cousin drove me to the hospital, but Clay followed us there. After they stitched me up, I slipped out a side entrance and called a cab to bring me here. Pa means well, Miss Jenna. He just thinks Clay has some growin' up to do. Anyway, the taxi driver and I were high school friends. I trust him not to tell anyone where he brought me, not even my ma."

Jenna's voice squeaked a little as she asked, "Has your daddy seen you?"

The young woman shivered and answered, "No. Clay doesn't let me out after a beating. I was able to slip away last time because he left the picnic with friends."

"Get in my car and lay Josh on the back seat. I'll be right back." Jenna ran into the house and bagged plastic utensils, two plastic bowls, and foods that did not need refrigeration or cooking. On the way out, she grabbed the jar of sun tea off her back porch. In the garage, she loaded the food into the trunk and threw in two sleeping bags. *I should call Sergeant Harley back and tell him what Clay's done to Callie, but I'm still hiding a body and don't need the police coming here!*

"Miss Jenna?"

She faced the perspiring young woman and asked, "Do you want to go to the police, Callie? I can drive you there."

"No, no, no, no! I'd have to tell them that my own father helped Clay find me."

"Sergeant Harley's a good man, Callie."

"Clay swears he can tell lies to get Josh taken away from me, and I can't take that chance."

"Then we need a way to keep you and Josh safe without turning my home into the O.K. Corral." When Callie hesitated, Jenna added, "I'm asking you to trust me."

Nodding, Callie slipped into the back seat with Josh, who hugged her without saying a word.

Jenna pulled back out of the garage, hitting the button to close it. Then she followed a dirt road into the woods. Having walked and driven the land most of her life, she knew where to turn at each of several forks and did not stop until she came to the cabin near a small lake.

"How long has it been since anyone used this place?" Callie asked.

"More than thirty years ago, we all came: Ronan, my father, your grandfather, your mother, and me. We hunted and fished here with Finn and Liam. Now, I've given it to Marcus."

"Will he mind my coming here—? Wait! My mother hunted and fished?"

Jenna chuckled. "He won't mind, and yes and no on your mother. She came, but she sunbathed while Liam and Finn fished with me, and she didn't hunt either. Carol Ann only came because she wanted to be with her father."

"She talks like she hated him."

"Not when we were young. Now, let me go in first and see if it's safe for Josh."

The steps and porch were swept, and the windows were cleaned. The door was solid on new hinges. Inside, Marcus had cleaned the large stone fireplace in the living room-kitchen area. Toward the back were three doors and an archway. She opened the French doors on the left to find a new bed with the tags still on it. It was in pieces, and the mattress was wrapped in plastic. She recognized the dresser and end tables as ones she had given Marcus permission to take from the Victorian.

Jenna opened the French doors to the right to find the second bedroom swept and almost emptied. The only things in there were a desk and chair that were in Kathleen's library before the reorganization. She opened the third door to find new fixtures in the bathroom. Jenna turned the faucet, and clean water streamed out. The sparkling toilet flushed. She smiled and thought, *Marcus has been busy, but when on earth did he find time*? Jenna closed the door and went through the archway.

The mudroom was still there with its large basin. She remembered her father and his friends rinsing all their dirty clothes in that basin before hanging them on a line outside. A sharp vision of her dad, who had died eight years before his friends, tightened his daughter's chest and moistened her eyes. After Matteo was gone, Ronan and Grady had included Jenna and Lia in all family activities.

Swiping at her tears, Jenna went to survey the kitchen. Marcus had refinished the butcher block counters, and all the wood smelled of lemon oil. The sink worked, but in place of the stove and the refrigerator, new wires and plumbing poked out of the wall.

Jenna returned to the car. "It's been cleaned and has running water. The generator must be working because the power is on, too. Bring in a sleeping bag and Josh. Settle him in the office, and I'll bring in everything else."

Callie hesitated.

"Listen, honey, even if your mother mentioned this cabin to your husband—and I can't imagine that—I doubt he could find it."

Callie nodded and slung the diaper bag strap over her good shoulder. She carried a bedroll while urging Josh up the steps ahead of her. Jenna made two trips to bring in the other bedroll and the bags of food. Inside, she sectioned oranges and mixed them with canned pineapple, marshmallows, and walnuts. She had just finished when Callie came out of the bedroom, smiling, and announced, "He fell asleep before I finished rolling out the sleeping bag."

"Besides this stuff, I packed bread and peanut butter, fresh fruit, jarred foods, and canned goods, some crackers and cookies, and some odds and ends like olives and pickles."

"How long are y'all expecting us to stay?"

Jenna shook her head and answered, "I have no idea. But, if Clay called your mother searching for you, Carol Ann will worry."

"She can't know where I am. She'll tell Pa, and he'll tell Clay — again!"

Callie sat at the table that Jenna had set with paper plates, napkins, and plastic utensils.

Jenna brought over a tall thermos filled with ice cubes, explaining, "I brought it from home, and it's melting, but still cold."

Callie placed ice chips in a napkin and pressed it against the cut and bruised side of her face. The two women nibbled at the almost-ambrosia.

"Could I get your mother up here without your father knowing?"

Callie adjusted the ice pack and said, "You knew her as a kid, but I've grown up with the crazy adult. Every time Pa starts to reminisce about school, she yells at him to forget the past. She's usually so drunk she can barely stand. It's pathetic."

"That's harsh, Callie."

"Miss Jenna, she locked my gram in that nursing home before she had to and told the staff not to let me in to see her. Ma keeps saying, 'Your gram and the devil; there's no tellin' them two apart.' When I ask Ma about her pa, she says, 'Your gramps is wherever he is, so let it go. If you had more brains, you'd still be a complete idiot.' Nice, huh, for her to say that to me in front of Josh?"

"Were you close to Belle when you were little?"

"Hell no!" She winced, then continued. "My gram Belle is a porcupine. Anyone who tries to be close to her ends up bleeding. I just need to understand why we're three generations of crazy. If I understood, I could save Josh from it." She wrapped more ice chips in a new napkin and pressed it against her stitched lip. "Whatever y'all do," Callie continued, "don't put your land up for sale."

"Why not?"

"Ma told Pa that everything connected to the past should burn, including Miss Kathleen's estate."

"She'd buy it just to burn it?"

Callie groaned and said, "Pa says Gram was real jealous of Miss Kathleen. I think Ma caught the hate like the flu." A cry from the child stopped the conversation. "I should take the medicine the doctor gave me and go in with Josh. My arm hurts, my face hurts, and I should sleep for a week, but Josh needs me."

"One question, Callie."

"Yes, Miss Jenna?"

"Wouldn't the doctor report all these beatings?"

The young woman's face flushed, and she stammered, "Until my...my cousin drove me to the hospital today, Clay always took me to his uncle; he's a vet."

"Damn it, Callie."

"I...I know."

"Okay. Take in the other sleeping bag for a cushion or blanket. I'll leave soon. There are bears in these woods, and you're injured, so I'll send Marcus back to help with firewood. He can stay the night." She started to turn away and stopped to say, "Oh, Callie, Carol Ann wouldn't shoot an animal or hook a fish. She came to be with her father because she loved him. No matter what happened to change her, that's the girl I knew."

Callie gave her a tired smile and ducked into the bedroom. As Jenna cleaned the kitchen, she heard Callie soothing her child.

Driving home, Jenna thought, *Kathleen, you're looking more innocent every day*. Back in the house, she pulled Marcus aside and told him about Callie. "I hope it's okay that I brought her there, and I'm hoping you can stay with them because of Callie's broken arm."

"You did the right thing. I'll pack a cooler with ice and with milk for Josh. I cleaned up the grill by the lake, so I'll grab some hot dogs and chopped meat for burgers, too."

After Marcus left. Jenna spent a moment to be grateful the twins were already in bed. Any worry about telling Anthony, or fear that he might go after Clay, needed to wait until morning.

Jenna dragged herself into the library and lit a fire. Then she curled up on the couch with the phone from her desk. Using the number on a business card, she dialed Carol Ann's cell phone.

CHAPTER 8
WRITING IN THE FUTURE TENSE

Carol Ann answered Jenna's call. "Callie! Callie, is that you?"

"No, it's Jenna."

"Jenna?"

"I'm sorry it's so late, but — if Billy is there, please pretend that I'm saying, 'I'm sorry, but Callie isn't at my house.'"

Carol Ann turned from the phone and yelled, "It's Jenna. She's sorry, but Callie isn't at her house." Back into the phone, she asked, "Jenna? Why are you callin'?"

"Carol Ann, you need to be careful what you say because Billy might repeat it to Clay."

She sounded uncertain but said, "Okay."

"Tomorrow morning, around seven, meet me at police headquarters — without Billy. I might have something I can tell you."

"Pol — oh. Why there?"

"If Clay follows either of us, I want to take him where he belongs."

Carol Ann growled into the phone. "Are you trying to organize my life like it is something in one of your books?"

"Try to sleep. I've heard she's safe for tonight."

After one sob, Carol Ann hung up.

Jenna went upstairs and set her alarm for six to give herself time to shower.

The next morning, she left before the twins were awake and arrived at police headquarters to find Carol Ann pacing around her red Audi A4. Jenna parked and walked over.

"You heard she's safe?" Carol Ann blurted out.

"I'll explain on the way. I need to drive us in your car, but the car will take a beating."

"I don't care."

Jenna knew how to drive a stick but had never driven an expensive car. With exaggerated care, she eased out of the parking lot and into traffic that would be considered light anywhere except their small town.

"You're leaving your car here?"

Jenna nodded and said, "Sergeant Harley said I could."

"What can you tell me about my daughter?"

"I have a few questions first, and then I need to make a phone call."

"Who the hell are you to ask me questions?"

"The one who might be able to bring you to Callie. But I need to know she'll be safe."

"What right do—?"

Jenna pulled the car into a coffee shop parking lot, saying, "I need a latte." Carol Ann frowned but followed her. They ordered at the counter and sat in a back booth. While they waited, Jenna said, "Your family put me in the middle of this mess when Clay showed up drunk at my house."

"Why your house?"

"I don't know. Maybe he heard that Callie and Anthony were at the picnic together. All I know is your daughter can get hurt worse if *we* — you and me — handle this wrong."

Carol Ann protested, "You think all this cloak and dagger shit helps?" She cut herself off when the barista called for pick up.

Jenna brought back an iced tea for Carol Ann and a hot chai tea latte for herself.

As soon as Jenna sat across from her again, Carol Ann lowered her voice to say, "You're acting like I hurt *my own* daughter."

"Let's pretend we're still friends, and I have to be honest. You do hurt your daughter — when you let Billy tell Clay where she is, and every time you act like Belle."

The vibration in Carol Ann's hand splashed iced tea on the table.

Jenna pulled napkins from the dispenser and cleaned the spill. Then she said, "I've heard you insult Callie the way your mother insults you."

"I'm getting madder than a cat in a dogfight!"

"Five seconds with the two of you at the town picnic let me see your mother in you. I hope there's enough Carol Ann left to help

Callie and Josh."

"You have balls talkin' to me like this."

"Yeah, my family knows how to make them."

Carol Ann's lips trembled.

Jenna added, "But we can soften our edges, my friend."

"You call this softened?"

"Hell, yes—you remember me worse. Anyway, I'll try to bring you and Callie together as long as you're not bringing your Belle side." *Stop talking,* Jenna told herself, *and give her a chance to breathe.* She waited, sipping her latte and wondering what Carol Ann knew about the skeleton on Kathleen's land.

"Find out if you can bring me to my daughter: just me. I'll try not to be my mother."

Jenna dialed her phone, saying, "Fair enough." When Callie answered, Jenna pretended she was talking to someone else. "I'm with Carol Ann," she said, "and she wants to know if she can see Callie."

Carol Ann's mouth began to open, but Jenna held a finger toward the woman's lips. When the distraught mother leaned back in her seat, Jenna said into the phone, "She loves her daughter and wants to start over. She'll come without Billy or Clay knowing about it." Hearing Callie's answer, she clicked off the call and said, "I can take you to her."

"This time, I'll drive. You're grinding the gears."

"Okay." Back in the car, Jenna gave directions as needed.

Within fifteen minutes, Carol Ann said, "We're headed toward your house."

"Past it."

"The cabin?"

"Yes."

Carol Ann groaned. "I can already hear my mechanics weeping." On the logging road to the cabin, the Audi crunched in and out of deep ruts and holes. "I hope wrecking my car isn't revenge because I'm rich," Carol Ann said.

"I've never cared about your money, but I do have a question."

"Another one? What is it?"

"Back when we were friends, you never talked to me about your father leaving. Why?"

Red-faced and swallowing a sob, Carol

Ann said, "I had to block it all out to keep from going even crazier than I did." She sank into a cold silence. As a branch dragged over the Audi's roof, she only winced. Finally, parked in front of the cabin, she sighed with relief.

"One more thing, Carol Ann. Sergeant Harley's a good guy. He'd be on Callie's side."

Before Carol Ann could respond, Marcus came out of the house with his jacket over his arm. Callie appeared behind him with Josh squeezing past her legs.

Carol Ann saw her daughter's injuries and gasped, "Oh, my God! Did Clay do that?" Tears ran down her cheeks, and she opened her arms. "I'm so sorry, Callie, for everything. Sweet Lord, I'm so sorry."

As Callie took slow, halting steps into her mother's arms, Josh squeezed between them.

Marcus and Jenna walked to Michael and Anthony's car. Once inside, Marcus hissed, "The Audi! You had her drive the Audi here?"

"I planned on leaving them together, so she'll need her car."

"Wow! It looks like Harry Potter's Whumping Tree had at it."

"Call it a test of relative values. Speaking of relatives, I need to tell Anthony what's happening, and you need to be there for a big brother talk about temper-management."

Marcus bounced the twins' car over ruts and mumbled, "Damn! A new Audi."

When they pulled up to the Victorian, the phone inside was ringing. Jenna rushed inside.

"Where's my wife?"

After taking a moment to recognize the voice, Jenna said, "Hi, Billy."

"Is Carol Ann there?"

Staying calm, she answered, "No. Carol Ann's not here, and neither is Callie. Even if I knew where they were, I wouldn't tell you because you might tell Clay."

"A family needs to stay together! And that can't happen if you keep having Clay thrown in jail."

"Instead of yelling at me, Billy, you should buy flowers and candy for all the apologizing you have to do. Now, say goodbye." She hung up. Then, sinking into a sitting room armchair, she smiled up at Marcus and said, "I'm beat."

Marcus sighed and admitted, "Me

too. I'm going upstairs to nap—probably 'til morning. I don't know how anyone keeps up with a two-year-old!"

Jenna went to her computer and found a note from Michael and Anthony that they were out. "Good," she said, and sat to type a letter. After proofing it three times, she laminated it and put it in a Ziplock bag. Then she collected a full-size shovel and a watering pail and hiked to the grave.

Jenna knelt by the skeleton and guessed where the chest might be. She used her hands to move a little dirt at a time until she reached leather. Then she laid the baggy on top of the jacket and bent the arm, ignoring the cracking sounds, to rest the hand on the letter. Using the shovel, she replaced the dirt until the jacket, the hand, and the letter were covered.

Not satisfied, she scooped groundcovers and their roots and replanted them over and around the grave. During the next hours, she needed to rest twice. As a last step, she dipped the can in the stream and watered the transplants.

Aloud, she said, "Grady, you were a

kind and funny second father after mine died. I promise to tend your grave and help Carol Ann if she'll let me. But right now, I need to go home." She stared at the setting sun and remembered there were bears in the forest. Having a shovel did not make Jenna feel safe enough. Somber and tired, she headed back to the house.

Just before entering the Victorian, she glanced back toward the skeleton and imagined Kathleen saying, *Ah Jenna, my lovely, I think Grady's a secret best kept to ourselves.*

EPILOGUE
THE LETTER

Dear Digger,

I believe you've found Grady Delford. He was a wonderful, loving, hard-drinking man who ran his best friend, Ronan, off the road. That accident killed Ronan, Liam, and Finn, and destroyed Grady.

I have no doubt it was Grady's wife, Belle, who killed her husband and buried him on Ronan's estate to throw suspicion on Ronan's widow. Belle's daughter, Carol Ann, might know something or everything, but being Belle's daughter has been punishment enough. So, with the only real killer in a nursing home, I'm letting Grady and the MacKenna family rest in peace.

Now, it's your turn to decide what you'll do.

Thank You

Frances Applequist, author of the supernatural thriller, *Fangs, Claws, and Camouflage: Zombie Problems*, and the historical fiction for young adults, *Nathan Ross and the American Revolution*, now brings you a contemporary and human murder mystery. Frances has led a life as diverse as her writing topics. She has been a plumbing dispatcher, a decorating-house paint mixer, an electric car raceway board operator, a law office administrative assistant, a college English instructor, and more. Her only constants have been her love for family, her obsession with writing, and her need to customize her coffee. Frances's roster of wonderfully quirky family members and friends bolsters her fascination with irrepressible characters!